First Experiences

Penny goes to a Party

Written by **Lynne Gibbs**

Illustrated by **Michael Peterkin**

BRIMAX

One day, a special letter addressed to
'Miss Penny Jones' arrives at Penny's house.
"I wonder who it's from?" she asks.

Penny opens the envelope and reads the invitation inside. "My friend, Julie, has invited me to her birthday party!" says Penny, excitedly.

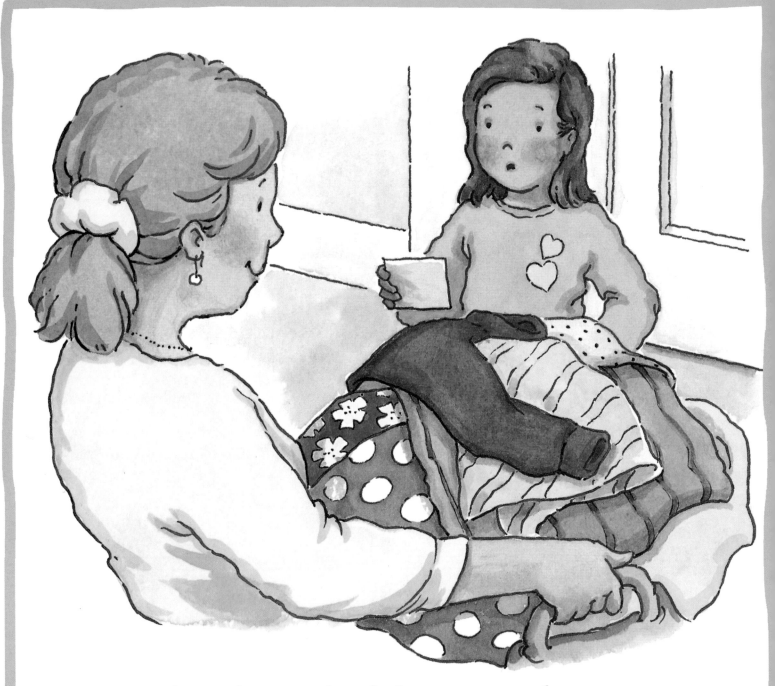

"But I don't have a birthday present for Julie... or a birthday card!" says Penny.

"Stop worrying!" laughs Penny's mother. "First you must write to Julie, accepting your party invitation. I will help you to write a note."

"Can we go shopping now?" asks Penny, as she finishes her note to Julie. "OK, let's go!" says Penny's mother, holding out her hand.

After looking at all the toys and books in a store, Penny was confused. "There is so much to choose from!" she says.

"I think Julie will like this book best," says Penny's mother. "So do I!" says Penny, as they pay for Julie's gift.

Next, Penny and her mother choose a card for Julie. "Happy birthday to a special friend," says Penny. "That's perfect!"

"Is that all we need to buy for Julie?" asks Penny. "No, we still need to get wrapping paper and a gift tag," says her mother.

"I'm sure we've forgotten something, you know," says Penny's mother. "Have we?" asks Penny. "Oh, dear! I wonder what it can be?"

"Now I remember!" smiles Penny's mother. "We haven't bought you a new dress to wear for Julie's party!" "Yippee!" says Penny.

"Oh, this one is beautiful!" says Penny, trying on
a pretty dress. "Let me see you twirl round," laughs
her mother.

"All that shopping has made me tired. Let's go home," says Penny's mother, at last. "Can I try on my new dress when we get home?" asks Penny. "Maybe," smiles her mother.

Back home, Penny's mother helps her to wrap Julie's book in the special birthday paper. Then they add the gift tag and a yellow bow.

All I have to do now is write a birthday message inside Julie's card," says Penny. "Ahh, I know what I'll say..."

Happy Birthday
to a special friend

On the day of Julie's birthday party, Penny felt nervous. "I hope Julie likes the present I've bought for her, and I wonder if I'll know any of the other children?" says Penny.

"Everything will be fine," says her mother, dropping Penny off at the party. And it was! "Come in and meet everyone, Penny," says Julie.

Penny soon makes friends with the other children.
"My name is Lisa, and this is Anna... and this is
Danny," says one little girl. "Hello, I'm Penny,"
smiles Penny.

Penny is pleased when Julie says, "Thank you for my present, Penny. How did you know that I've wanted this book for ages?"

It's soon time for the games to begin – and Penny
wins the prize for standing perfectly still like a statue.

There are party balloons, streamers, poppers, whistles and lots of yummy food to eat.

There is even a funny clown to entertain them!

"Julie's party was great – and I made lots of new friends!" says Penny, later. "And I've been invited to two more parties next week!"
"More presents to buy!" laughs her mother.